For Tom ~ D B

*For Lisa, Tony, and their little bears
Morgan and Macy ~ C P*

Copyright © 2009 by Good Books, Intercourse, PA 17534
International Standard Book Number: 978-1-56148-656-4

Library of Congress Catalog Card Number: 2008033192

Text copyright © David Bedford 2008
Illustrations copyright © Caroline Pedler 2008

Original edition published in English by Little Tiger Press,
an imprint of Magi Publications, London, England, 2008.

Printed in China

Library of Congress Cataloging-in-Publication Data

Bedford, David, 1969-
Little Bear's big sweater / David Bedford ;
illustrated by Caroline Pedler.

p. cm.

Summary: When Big Bear reluctantly hands down his favorite sweater
and Little Bear soils it, the brothers learn to overcome their differences.
ISBN 978-1-56148-656-4 (pbk. : alk. paper)

1. Brothers--Fiction. 2. Sharing--Fiction. 3. Sweaters--Fiction.
I. Pedler, Caroline, ill. II. Title.

PZ7.B3817995Li 2009
[E]--dc22

2008033192

Little Bear's Big Sweater

David Bedford   Caroline Pedler

Good Books

Intercourse, PA 17534
800/762-7171
www.GoodBooks.com

Big Bear loved his stripy sweater. It was warm. It was soft. And it was his very favorite.

But it was getting harder and harder to put on.

"It's too small for you!" said Little Bear, giggling.

"It's not," said Big Bear. "It fits just right!"

Mom laughed. "I think it's time I knitted you a new sweater, Big Bear. Why don't you give that one to your brother?"

"But it's too big
for him," said
Big Bear.
"No it's not,"
said Little Bear.

He pulled it quickly
over his head.
"It fits just right!"

"You better take good care of it,"
said Big Bear. "It's my favorite
sweater – EVER."

"I will," said Little Bear, happily.
"It's my favorite ever, too!"

Off they ran together
to play. "Now I look just
like you!" cried Little Bear.

Big Bear gave his brother a piggyback ride through the tall grass. Little Bear chuckled as he was jiggled about.

The two brothers jumped through the puddles with a

Splish!

Splash!

Splosh!

"This is fun!" said Big Bear.

Then Big Bear climbed
along a high branch.
"I'm climbing too!"
said Little Bear.
"You're pulling me
down," cried his
brother. "Get off!"

"I can wibble-wobble
like you!" said Little Bear.
"Stop it!" said Big
Bear. "You're wobbling
too much!"
And suddenly . . .

. . . Crack! went the log,
as it split in two.
Sploosh!

went the bears as they landed
in a muddy puddle.

"Look what you've done!" yelled Big Bear. "You've broken the wobbly log. And you've made a mess of MY sweater!"

Little Bear looked down at
the soggy sweater. His lip
began to tremble.

"I'm s-o-r-r-y!" he said,
and he ran away into the
woods.

"Good riddance," said Big
Bear, grumpily. "It's better
playing on my own."

Big Bear slid down the slippery-slidey
slope. He chased a butterfly until
he was dizzy. Then he sat on
the end of the see-saw.
But with only one
bear, it wouldn't
go up or down.

Playing is no fun
without Little Bear,
he thought. And he
began to feel very
lonely.
"Where are you,
Little Bear?"

Big Bear searched
the places Little Bear
liked the most. He
looked everywhere.
But he wasn't
in the hollow
honey tree . . .

or in their den
in the bush . . .

He wasn't even hiding under
the big rock.
Little Bear wasn't anywhere!
Where could he have
gone all on
his own?

Suddenly, Big Bear saw a woolly thread. So he followed it quickly through the trees, around a bush and deeper and deeper into the woods, until at last he found . . .

. . . a very sad and
lonely Little Bear.

"I've ruined our favorite ever sweater!" Little Bear cried when he saw Big Bear.

Big Bear gave his brother a big hug. "Don't worry," he said, kindly. "It's only a sweater! I'm sorry I shouted at you."

"It's all right," Little Bear sniffed. "I shouldn't have run off without you."

Big Bear took him by the hand. "Let's go home," he said.

On the way back,
Big Bear wrapped
up all the wool
into a ball.

"We had a little accident,"
he told Mom when they
got home.
　"Poor Little Bear!"
said Mom. "Don't worry,
I know just what to do."

The very next morning,
Big Bear and Little Bear
had the best surprise . . .
two brand new, matching,
stripy sweaters!

"Now I can be just like
you, Little Bear!" said
Big Bear. "You're the best
brother EVER!"